MARTHA
and the
BUNNY
BROTHERS

I ♥ School

Clara Vulliamy

HarperCollins *Children's Books*

For the real
Martha
with love

First published in hardback by
HarperCollins Children's Books in 2012
First published in paperback in 2012

1 3 5 7 9 10 8 6 4 2

ISBN: 978-0-00-741917-3

HarperCollins Children's Books is a division
of HarperCollins Publishers Ltd.

Text and illustrations copyright © Clara Vulliamy 2012

The author/illustrator asserts the moral right to be
identified as the author/illustrator of the work.
A CIP catalogue record for this title is available from
the British Library.

Visit our website at:
www.harpercollins.co.uk

Printed in China

This is a
happy book all about
MARTHA –

that's me!

A few very important things about me, just so you know…

my **favourite** colour is **yellow**

and my favourite lolly is **pink**...

I like

d👀dling

and scootering

doing my own biscuits

and

and trampolining…

I **love** my snowdome

and my starry sunglasses

(because I like to see the world all rosy!)

but my yellow-and-blue-and-orange-and-pink spotty wellies are what

I love best!

I **never** take them off, not even in bed!

News!
Today is my first day at school!

I am very excited about starting school, but there is one **huge** problem...

my bunny brothers!

Here's Monty.
His favourite colour is red
and he's crazy about robots
and rockets
and dinosaurs.
He's always full of beans and
he talks **all the time**!

And here's Pip.
He's the baby.
He doesn't say much.

They will both really miss me!

Oh, and this is our puppy, Paws.

Of

all

the

pets

in

our

street,

Paws is **by far** the naughtiest.

But I'd better get ready – Mum is calling us for breakfast. She says, "Get a move on, Martha!"

"Sit down, Monty! Sit down, Pip!" I say. Mum says
I need a nice big breakfast for my first day at school!

I have   cereal   a banana   and orange juice

Monty has   toast   with jam   and apple juice

and Pip has   soldiers   an egg   and milk

Monty will only eat his breakfast inside his box and Pip
is squeezing egg through his fingers. "Mud!" says Pip.

What *funny bunnies* they are!

And now I'm getting dressed. I want to wear something **very special** for school but I don't know what to choose...

they are favourites! all my

Now I'm ready!

But wait – best of all I have
a **fantastic** new school bag!
Inside it has one big pocket
and lots of little pockets to put
all my things in.

"What's that, Martha?"
says Monty.

I say, "It's my new
school bag."

Monty says,
"Can we go to school, too?
Me and Pip and Paws?
We can go in your bag –
we can squeeze up small!"

"But you are still little. One day you will be big enough,"
I say, "but today only **ME** is just the right size for school."

Once I was
very little

then I was
little

and now I am
BIG

Sometimes I think about what I'd like to do when I'm huge...

make hats

and drive a bus

and be a diver

and have a
cake shop

and be a vet

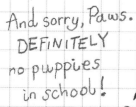

And sorry, Paws.
DEFINITELY
no puppies
in school!

My bunny brothers are looking really sad.

"But what will we do, Martha, while you are at school?" says Monty.

Luckily, I have a brilliant idea. Let's set up the

Happy Bunny Club!

"Hooray!" shouts Monty.
"Hooray!" shouts Pip.
"Hooray, hooray!" shouts Monty.

"...What is a club?"

"It's a very exciting thing that you are **in**," I say.

"Like a box?" says Monty.

"A **bit** like a box, but not completely," I say, "and it happens in a **SECRET DEN!**"

The **DEN** needs:

comfy cushions

Monty's toys

Pip's zebra

games

music

apples for a snack

Sorry, Paws, no puppies in the club. You'd make a mess!

"Squash!" says Pip.

"It's not
a squash,"
says Monty.
"It's cosy!"

"Do you like it?
Are you happy?"
I say.
"**GREAT!**"

Now I need to get ready for school because Mum is calling, **"Ten minutes** to go, Martha!"

But Monty says, "Don't go – we need a sign for the den!"

So I make a sign and do my best grown-up writing.

It says,

Happy Bunny Club
that is fun and games
for two left-behind bunnies

This bit was chewed by Paws

Now I start packing my bag for school.
I choose a few of my favourite things to take...

I've had this bear since I was JUST BORN!

one or two books   my recorder   my old bear

some   of   my   smaller   ornaments

and **of course** my snowdome

and
my

starry
sunglasses.

Now
my
bag is a **bit full.**

But the little  bunnies still follow me everywhere.

 "Are those my fairy wings, Monty?"

"No, these aren't your fairy wings, Martha," says Monty.

"These are my super-speedy-flyers for going all around the world!

I **need** them for the club!"

I need my **best bits and pieces**
from my making box to fill my bag,
but I don't know what to choose...

they are **all** my best!

Paws, come back here
with that ribbon!

Now my bag is **very full**...

Here are the little bunnies – **AGAIN.**

Monty says, "We need a special badge to show we are in the *Happy Bunny Club.*"

"Too busy!" I say.

"Please!" says Monty.

"Peas!" says Pip.

So I make a badge for Monty...

and a badge for Pip.

"Now I really must get ready, little bunnies!" I say.

I **need**

a pencil,  and a ruler

a rubber for my pencil case,

but when I look for my best pens... they've completely disappeared!

you

got

"Have

my in

pens

best there?"

I say.

Happy Bunny Club
that is fun and games
for two left-behind bunnies

"No, we don't have them, Martha," says Monty.

"I really **need** them for school," I say,

but there's no time because Mum is saying,

"Five minutes, Martha!"

Quick! **I must hurry!**

I need…

my coat!

My scarf!

My gloves!

Just a **few** more things!

My crown!

My armbands!

My torch!

Now my
bag is
too full
to do up the zip.

Luckily
I have
lots of
pockets!

But –
Squeeze!

I can't fit through the front door.

Mum says,
"Crumbs, Martha – you can't take all that stuff to school!"

I don't know what to do...

Today is my first day at school
and I can't even take all my favourite things.
And where are my bunny brothers?

"Martha, Martha, we made **this** for you – it's your Happy Bunny Club Badge!"

I love it!

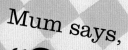

Mum says,

"One more minute, Martha!"

So I unpack my bag and I put in my Happy Bunny Club Badge. It's all I really need.

"You can look after my snowdome, Pip," I say,

"and you can look after my starry sunglasses, Monty."

"I know you will really miss me, little bunnies," I say, "but be brave!"

Happy Bunny Club
that is fun and games
for two left-behind bunnies

"And look after the den until I get home!"

While I'm at school having **fun**, I know my bunny brothers are…

waiting…

waiting…

waiting…

until –

"I'm back!"

They go **mad** with joy to see me!

"I love school,"

I tell them, "and I got lots of great stuff...

kind helper

great work!

But look – I've still got my Happy Bunny Club Badge!

Let's go into the den!"

I squash up with my
bunny brothers because…

…I know they can't really have a

Happy Bunny Club

without…

me!

"But what shall we do about Paws?" says Monty. "He is **desperate** to join in!"

Luckily, Happy Bunnies never leave anyone out, so I say...

"OK, Paws, you **can** join the club!"

The End!